LIFELESS LIFE

"I KNEW IF IT WAS TRUE, NOTHING IN THE WORLD COULD STOP HIM FROM COMING TO ME."

AARCHI ADVANI SAINI

I'd like to dedicate my work to my Father. Not because he is the one who inspire me, but because he is the one who supported me for what I'm. He is none other than Sanjeev Advani.

Mr. Sanjeev Advani Saini

For the sake of Father, my Creator, and my Master, My great teacher, and messenger, who taught me the purpose of life. Who never stop giving of themselves in countless ways, who leads me through the valley of darkness with the light of hope and support, who stands by me when things look bleak, whom I can't force myself to stop loving.

Contents

"author"

Aarchi Advani Saini.!
   [ ] Author of the book "The Loads Of Poetry"
[ ] Social media "Aarchi Advani Saini"
[ ] Aries, believe in destiny.

Aarchi Advani Saini.!

Aarchi was born in India on 25th March 2002, the daughter of Sanjeev Advani Saini and his wife Mamta Saini.

She becomes one of the youngest author of the hometown Shamli. So renowned for "The loads of poetry). She has sold the book worldwide, the recipient of numerous prestigious awards in her writing journey. She writes daily columns syndicated throughout the world. Aarchi Advani is well known for her writing on many other platforms. And overthrowing mankind. She is also a fantasy and literary fiction author specializing in "Life".

The Aarchi Advani also hosts a channel where she uses her passion for storytelling. And a background in business to help other creatives navigate their writing. And publishing journey. When she's not writing or tubing she enjoys listening to books,

Making stories on her own. And love to live in her virtual world.

CHAPTER ONE

THE FANCY WORD FOR A NOT-SO-FANCY CONDITION, RIGHT?

It was a sunny day in my mundane life, an unusually sunny day. Sitting in the passenger seat of my father's car, I shielded my eyes from the scorching sun, the heat leaving tiny drops of sweat alongside my chin. It bad day for the air conditioner to stop working, I think.

Naturally, I found myself cursing the weather, although I had prayed for it just last night. It had been raining constantly for the past one week and being someone very emotionally inclined to the weather, I had my fair share of outbursts for the past few days. Seasonal dysthymia was a thing.

The fancy word for a not-so-fancy condition, right?

Traffic was not on our side either. We had been stuck in a small yet disturbingly slow line of cars and bikes for the past ten minutes.

"I'm so thirsty", my father whined.

I was thirsty too. It would be another twenty minutes before we reach home, not to mention I had asked for the longer, scenic route. I cursed myself under my breath.

But just then from the corner of my eyes, I saw something. A familiar figure leaning over a vehicle parked by the side of the road. He was not alone. Another masked man was talking to him, they laughed, and I imagined I heard it. A smile crept along my lips behind my mask, and suddenly I was thankful for it.

Ever since the virus took over our lives, I'd been having my fun imagining what people looked like behind their covered faces. And more than often, I would come across someone who looked like Ron. It had been five years since I last saw him, heard him laugh. Five years since my father told me about the accident.

I ran my eyes along the length of his figure, he was about the same height as Ron, same dark complexion. He seemed happy. He was dressed in a white and blue striped tshirt and blue jeans. Now this was the tricky part. Ron always wore solid colors you see, plain blacks or greys. Never stripes .Nothing vibrant. Even though he was the most vibrant person I'd ever met. There was no one like him, we were so different. I think he knew that. Truth is, it scared the hell out of me. I knew I couldn't keep up with him. In the end, he had to leave me behind. Who could blame him? I was just holding him back.

Once in a while, I'd imagine what he would say to me if he was alive. Would he notice how short my hair was? Or that I stopped wearing skirts? Would he comment on my weight? Probably. But nothing too mean, he had a way of being sarcastically funny. And I would laugh, not because it was funny, but just because I wanted to laugh with him again. I missed hearing our voices in collision. It had been five years after all.

Just then, I felt a sudden jolt of pain in my chest and I realised my eyes had welled up. Thankfully the cars had started moving so my father hadn't noticed.

But the boy standing infront of me, leaning over his vehicle, had.

The pain in my chest grew as I saw him fixated on me, looking at me, or through me. He let his one hand slide his mask down and I saw his face in the side mirror as we drove ahead. It had been five years since I'd seen Ron. Five years since I'd heard him laugh. Five years since he saw me cry as the car drove away for the second time, today.
TO BE CONTINUED.

CHAPTER TWO

"ARE YOU TAKING YOUR PILLS?"

"You're awfully quiet", my father shrugged as he parked the car in our driveway twenty minutes later.

"Just tired", I muttered, as I hurry into the house and into my room. I plopped on the bed and drew the blanket over my head. 'Shit. I just saw Ron'. My head hurt just thinking about it.

Two knocks and my mother walked in. "All okay ?"

I sighed. My parents always took everything so seriously. I wish they'd get off my back for once.

"Just a headache, I'm fine"
"Are you taking your pills?"

I straightened, preparing to snap at her, but decide against it. I had too much on my plate right now.

"Yes, mom. You know very well that I do".

I've always been bad at taking my medicine and my parents had developed this method of making me take it after dinner in front of them. I guess this is what happens when both your parents are doctors. For every sneeze, you got a pill or worse, a shot.

She sighed and walked out, closing the door behind her.

I couldn't just wait around in my room doing nothing, I had to talk to Ron's sister about this. She was the only one who'd believe me.

I dial in the number on my cell.

"Lisa, it's me, Mia"

Silence.

"Wow, I haven't heard from you in a while", she finally said.

"Yeah, sorry about that. It was hard to stay in touch. You know how it was".

"Yeah, of course. What's up?"

"I...I just saw Ron. You were right all along, he's here, in this town!".

More silence.

"You saw him? When ?"

"Today, at the bus stop. We were stuck in traffic and he was with a friend I guess".

"Which friend?"

"I didn't see", I paused. "But, he saw me. He saw me, Lisa. He took off his mask when he saw me like he wanted me to see him", I shuddered.

"Mia, what are you going to do?"

"I need to see him. I have to talk to him. We have to find him, Lisa, don't you want to see your brother ? Gosh how long has it been?"

I heard Lisa sigh over the phone and felt my brows curl.

"Can we please talk before we go looking for him?", She said finally. "I'll meet you at Bert's Cafe in two hours. Please".

I think for a second, utterly disappointed at her lack of excitement but finally agree. Hanging up the phone, I lay back on my bed, lost in all things Ron. Five years, it had been five years since I last saw him. My parents weren't too fond of his impulsive, rebellious nature. He always had these crazy ideas, almost all of which could easily land him in trouble. He'd miss out on classes for weeks to go camping with his friends or mountain biking. And when I started slacking off in my academics, my father had a talk with Ron about our future together. He wanted to live on the edge and I'd always been afraid of falling, up until Ron happened.

Sure enough, I drifted off to sleep and when I woke up, Lisa was staring at me, a man standing beside her.

I couldn't believe my eyes. I sat up in my bed, unable to control the tears.

"When Lisa told me, I had to come to see you", he said. TO BE CONTINUED.

CHAPTER THREE

"I'M COMING FOR YOU"

Five years ago.

"Do that thing with your tongue again ", I smiled, cozying up to Ron who was lying shirtless beside me. We had dumped his mattress on the floor and flooded it with pillows and blankets. Forging forts out of linen was our thing. Something like this would've sounded silly to me before but with Ron, I could be a child all over again, without judgement.

Ron curled his tongue and leaned over for a kiss. As I accepted it, gingerly, he moved his one hand over my waist and pushed his weight down on me, laughing as he did so. Ah, the warmth of his skin against mine. Only when he was next to me, I'd realise how cold and lifeless I felt on my own. He was like my personal sun. He could breathe color into me with just one touch. I felt safe, saved even.

"You know, I think I want to drop out of college", he said, pulling back and lying on his arm. "There's so much I want to do. I can't do any of those things if I'm stuck in one place", he said tetchily.

I sighed. "I want to come with you, you know I'll come right".

Ron looked at me with those warm brown eyes and I melted once again. "You have six more weeks till you graduate. And then, we travel the world", he beamed. "I've got some cash saved up for us with my part-time job. Jack is taking me to a cabin up on the mountains, it's the perfect start. I leave this Saturday. Once I'm all set up, I'm coming for you".

I laid back on his arm, breathing life into his words and dreaming of a world where I would be his and he would be mine with nothing standing in our way. A world without planning and rationalizing, where we followed our guts instead of social norms that told us how to live the life of our dreams, where lovers could be lovers without reservation. And a house in the mountains sounded like just the place to start that dream.

To Be Continued.

CHAPTER FOUR

"I'D NEVER FELT MORE COLD AND LIFELESS IN MY LIFE."

Six weeks went by and my parents started sensing something strange about my behavior. I hadn't seen Ron in weeks and on top of that, I'd learned my father had tried to talk Ron into ending our relationship. I let it not get to my head, what did my father know of love anyway? He'd married the first woman his father approved of or rather could afford the hefty dowry that was promptly requested. That was the way of the world', my mother had told me. So basically my mother bought my father and was willingly offered as a scapegoat by her parents. The whole idea made me sick.

The cell service was bad where Ron was staying and his parents often called me worried sick ever since he left college. Ron didn't care for them, he was sick of watching his father drinking his life away and hitting his mother till he had to intervene. Once Ron pushed his father away and his mother slapped him for being an ungrateful child. Ron never stepped foot in that house again. He had come crying to me that day, the first time I ever saw him cry.

'It's not his fault, she's letting it happen to her, he'd told me. 'She doesn't want to be saved.

I wished I could tell Ron that most people felt like they didn't have a choice. Not everyone was brave like him. If they were, sex wouldn't be a forbidden word whispered in the shadows, and marriage wouldn't remain just a contract.

It had been a few days since I'd talked to Ron and there were reports of landslides in the area. I'd been in my room, glued to the phone, talking to all the Gods I knew when my father came in. 'A body has been found, he'd told me. I think for the first time I saw sympathy in my father's eyes, sympathy for my dead boyfriend sympathy for his grieving daughter, who was now as good as dead anyway

The world wasn't kind to people like Ron, who chose to see it in its most raw, unappealing self. It buries them alive, the body and the mind suffocating side by side as the papers scream bloody murder and feign support for the forsaken. I hated this world. I wanted to run away, and so I ran.

It took them five days to find me. I was covered in dirt, lying in a hole I had dug up myself, or so they assumed looking at my fingernails, covered in Ron's old clothes. They said I was trying to bury myself. I don't remember much of it. All I remember is waking up in a hospital bed, with all sorts of IVs and medications being pumped into my thin dry veins. I'd never felt more cold and lifeless in my life.

TO BE CONTINUED.

CHAPTER FIVE

"HOW DO YOU FEEL?" "FREE", I SMILED. "THANKYOU".

My stay at the hospital lasted for a week. Shortly after, I was informed there were multiple 'episodes' at the mention of Ron's death. I would try to run away in search of him, break the windows of my room when they tried to lock me in, cutting myself in the process, and losing so much blood that they found me unconscious when they rushed in.

I was in denial. For days on end, I would wait for a phone call or any news on the identification of the body that was found but there was none. Just a few locals claiming Ron used to live in that cottage that collapsed and that they hadn't seen him since. Surely he must've gotten away. The whole world had given up on him without any proof or evidence of his demise. How could I?

What followed was a series of drugs and therapy sessions with Dr. Anthony Marcus. I'd have to admit, whatever little comfort I got during those few months were from his sessions. He never questioned me or corrected me when I told him Ron was still out there. Most of our sessions we'd talk about the time I'd spent with Ron and how happy and free he'd made me. And over time, by reliving every memory I had of Ron, I grieved him till one day I knew I could wake up and face the truth. Ron was gone. That's exactly what they needed me to believe and so, that's what I told them.

"And that was our last session", Dr. Anthony had told me after a few months. "How do you feel?"

"Free", I smiled. "Thankyou".

"I'm glad to hear that. Now remember to take your pills daily and if you experience any more anxiety, don't hesitate to call".

"I won't", I lied. The pills were very uncomfortable. They gave me nausea and gastritis and often I'd hide them under my tongue and spit it out later. My parents always kept a close watch on me but I didn't try to do anything crazy again.

I hadn't seen Dr. Anthony for a long time. I was doing better, I graduated, got into college, even made a few friends. And if Ron was out there, he'd be happy for me. This is what Ron would've wanted. For me to move on.

To Be Continued.

CHAPTER SIX

"I KNEW IF IT WAS TRUE, NOTHING IN THE WORLD COULD STOP HIM FROM COMING TO ME."

The present.

I woke up, bewildered, that I'd been betrayed by someone I'd considered a friend. Dr. Anthony met my gaze with kind eyes, he knew I was hurting again. He knew I wasn't to be judged. I could hear my parents' hushed voices out in the corridor. Everything was falling apart. They would never let me find Ron. They were going to put me in a hospital bed and drug me until I forgot his name.

His name, that I'd thought a million times over in my head, his name that I'd tattooed to my collar bone, close to my heart. The thought of living a life where I couldn't say his name ached me, so much that I collapsed under his gentle gaze, once again, a victim to those kind eyes that seemed to read me perfectly.

When I came to, I was still in my bed, hooked onto an iv stand while Dr. Anthony adjusted the flow rate.

"Mia, how do you feel?"

"Like I just had a nightmare".

"It's normal to feel discouraged. But we'll have it under control in no time", he smiled. "You're a smart girl, you know how your brain can play tricks on you. We've talked about this."

I nodded. Maybe I was imagining it. Maybe it was all just a misunderstanding. As much as I wanted Ron to be alive, I knew if it was true, nothing in the world could stop him from coming to me.

"Now get some rest okay? Remember, lots of fluids. Just like last time", he waved as he stepped outside.

I sank back into my bed, thinking of the boy in traffic.'Ron would never wear that', I think to myself, my last attempt in calming my racing heart and eventually slipping into a dream where Ron has his arms around me, staring out of our cabin in the mountains, just like he'd promised.

Somewhere in the city, a boy in a striped tshirt and jeans was lost in thought, wondering where he'd seen the girl in the car.

"Dude, come on. We'll be late for work", his friend nudged him, yanking him back from thought.

"You sure I've never been in this town before?", Ron asked, "I thought I saw someone".

"Not that I know of. When we found you, you were pretty out of it. Head bashed in, blood everywhere. You wouldn't quit mumbling about some cabin up north".

"Right", Ron sighs.

"Who'd you see?"

"A girl", Ron chuckled nervously. "Way out of my league though".

"Come on Romeo, before you get us both fired", he laughed, starting the bike. Ron climbed on his back, turning one last time to look at where the car had been, before they took off and disappeared into traffic.